Happy 3rd Birthday to Nathan Jeremy
with love from Gran_____ Grandpa Ehlert

For Rebecca and Nina
M.M.

For Josh
L.C.

First published in 2001 in Great Britain by
Gullane Children's Books

Text © Miriam Moss 2001
Illustrations © Lynne Chapman 2001

This 2008 edition published by Sandy Creek
by arrangement with Gullane Children's Books
185 Fleet Street, London, EC4A 2HS, United Kingdom

Sandy Creek, 122 Fifth Avenue, New York, NY 10011

ISBN-13: 978-1-4351-0923-0

10 9 8 7 6 5 4 3 2 1

Printed and bound in Indonesia

I'll Be
Your Friend!

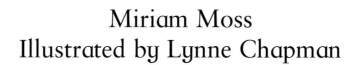

Miriam Moss
Illustrated by Lynne Chapman

SANDY CREEK

Smudge yawned herself awake in her new room in her new house. Stripe poked his head around the door. "How many days until my birthday?" asked Smudge. "One less than yesterday," replied Stripe, as he did every morning.

Suddenly Smudge sat up. "Then it's today!" she cried, jumping out of bed. "Happy Birthday!" smiled Stripe, handing Smudge her present. It was a beautiful paint set.

Downstairs, Smudge painted while Stripe cooked a delicious birthday breakfast. Suddenly Smudge put down her brush, looking worried.

"Who will come to my party?" she asked.
"I don't know anyone who lives around here."
"You'll soon make some friends," said Stripe,
"but we could have a special party this year,
just you and me."
Smudge tried to look pleased.
Quickly, Stripe added, "Perhaps we
could build a treehouse to have it in!"
Smudge's face lit up.

All morning, Smudge and Stripe worked hard. Smudge drew plans of the treehouse while Stripe sawed and hammered. By the afternoon the house was built. Stripe went to find a rug for the floor.

Smudge sat in the treehouse, waiting for Stripe.
However hard she tried, she couldn't help feeling
sad that she had no friends to play with on her
birthday. A tear fell to the ground, splosh!
Then another, splosh! Then another, splosh! splosh!

Suddenly something moved below.

"It's raining," said a voice.
Smudge peered down. Two bright eyes stared back.
"Hello," said Hare, climbing quickly up
the ladder. "I'm Hare, who are you?"
"Smudge," replied Smudge.
"What a lovely treehouse!"
remarked Hare.
"Is it yours?"

"Yes," said Smudge, wiping her eyes.
Hare looked at her more closely.
"Why are you crying?" he asked.
"We've just moved and it's my birthday
and I haven't got any friends to come to my party,"
Smudge said, all in a rush.
"I'll be your friend," said Hare. "And I've got
some other friends you can meet too. Come on!"

"Hello, Stripe, this is Hare, he's going to be my friend and he's got some other friends I can have too! Can we go and find them in my boat?" asked Smudge. "Of course," smiled Stripe. "Why don't you ask them to come and play in your new treehouse."

As they rowed off,
Hare spotted Goose.
"Upside down as
usual," remarked Hare.
"Hey, Goose! Turn
down-side-up!"
Goose popped up, her
mouth full of river weed.
"This is Smudge,"
said Hare.

"Hello, Fudge,"
said Goose.
"Smudge, not Fudge,"
corrected Hare.
"It's her birthday
and this is her boat.
She's got a treehouse
and we're all going
back there to play,"
said Hare. "Come on!"

Goose followed Smudge and Hare.
"Goose, have you seen Mole?" Hare called.
But before she could answer, a nose appeared
from an earthy volcano on the shore.
"Oh, look, there he is!" Hare cried.

"Who's that?" asked Mole, blinking in the light.
"It's me," called Hare, "and Goose, and this is Smudge.
It's her birthday and this is her boat. She's got
a treehouse and we're all going there to play."
"Hello, Smudge," said Mole. ". . . Oh, and
Happy Birthday!"

"Climb in, Mole!" said Hare.
"Oh no," said Mole. "I'm afraid
that boat is far too wobbly for me."
"Don't worry," said Hare. "You can
sit between us."
"It will still wobble, Hare," worried Mole.
"I promise, it will hardly wobble at all,"
insisted Hare.

At last Mole was persuaded to climb in
and the new friends set off for the treehouse.
"Race you down river, Goose!" shouted Hare.

They had almost reached the bank, when Thunk! Goose
bumped into the boat and the three friends flew backwards.
"You're all down-side-up!" Goose remarked.
"Oh, Goose!" laughed Hare, "You forgot to slow down!"

Poor Mole was shaking like jelly.
"Are you all right, Mole?" asked Smudge,
offering him a hand.
"I think so," said Mole, pushing his
glasses back on. But when he saw the
treehouse, Mole felt much better!

Inside the treehouse, Stripe had laid out a delicious lunch. There was even a birthday cake in the shape of a paint set!

The new friends sang Happy Birthday
to Smudge, ate their lunch and played games
until it was nearly dark.

That night, Stripe tucked a very happy Smudge into bed. "Did you have a nice day with your new friends?" asked Stripe.

But there was no answer.
Smudge was fast asleep.